The Joke is on Thomas

Based on a story by **Brian Swenlin**

Adapted by **Claire Sipi**

DEAN

First published in Great Britain 2023 by Dean, part of Farshore
An imprint of HarperCollins*Publishers*
1 London Bridge Street, London SE1 9GF
www.farshore.co.uk

HarperCollins*Publishers*
Macken House, 39/40 Mayor Street Upper,
Dublin 1, D01 C9W8, Ireland

Based on a story by Brian Swenlin
Adapted by Claire Sipi

Based on the Railway Series by The Reverend W Awdry.
©2023 Gullane (Thomas) Limited.
Thomas the Tank Engine & Friends™ and Thomas & Friends™
are trademarks of Gullane (Thomas) Limited.
©2023 HIT Entertainment Limited. HIT and the HIT logo are
trademarks of HITEntertainment Limited.

ISBN 978 0 0086 1748 6
Printed in China
001

A CIP catalogue record for this title is available from the British Library.

HIT entertainment   CREATED BY BRITT ALLCROFT

FSC
MIX
Paper | Supporting
responsible forestry
www.fsc.org   FSC™ C007454

This book is produced from independently certified FSC™ paper
to ensure responsible forest management.

For more information visit: www.harpercollins.co.uk/green

One day, Thomas, Sandy and Carly decided to play a joke on Percy.

Thomas winked at Sandy and turned to Percy.
"Hey, Percy, would you take one of those boxcars for me?"

"Of course," said Percy. He coupled up with the car, ready to help his friend.

"Where do you want it?" he asked.

"Actually, I've changed my mind. You can leave it right there," replied Thomas.

Percy pulled away from the car …

… **POP!** There was a loud bang and rainbow confetti shot out of the roof of the car, covering a startled Percy and landing in colourful heaps on the tracks.

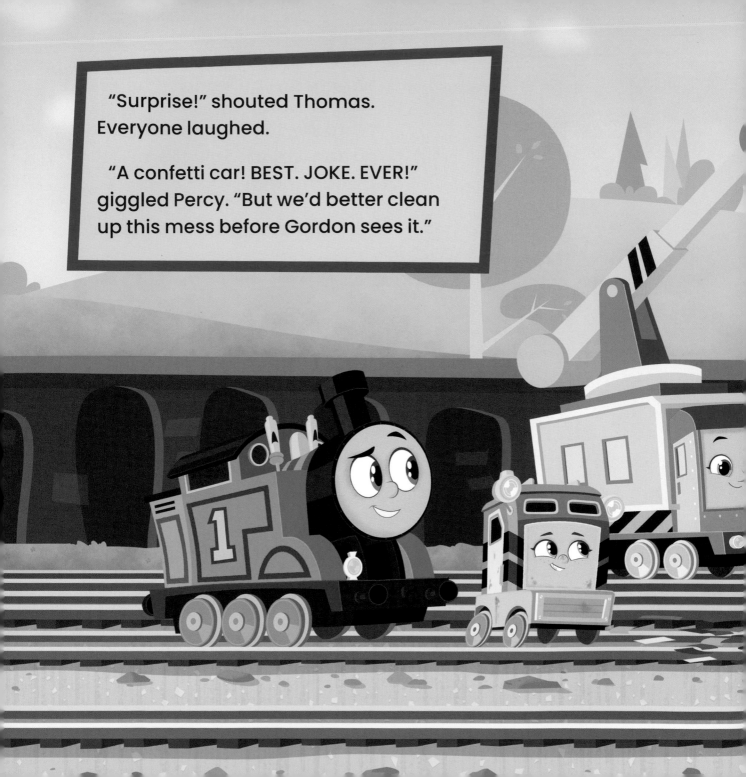

"Surprise!" shouted Thomas. Everyone laughed.

"A confetti car! BEST. JOKE. EVER!" giggled Percy. "But we'd better clean up this mess before Gordon sees it."

"Sees what?" asked Gordon, pulling up alongside the engines.

"Oh, hello, Gordon," replied Thomas sheepishly. "We were just being silly."

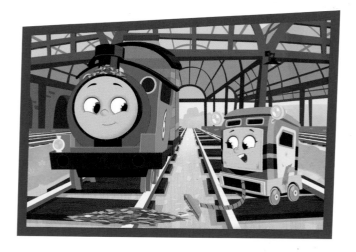

"Yes, I can see that. Very silly," chuckled Gordon.

"Don't worry, cleaning up the mess right now," cried Sandy, and she quickly vacuumed up all the confetti.

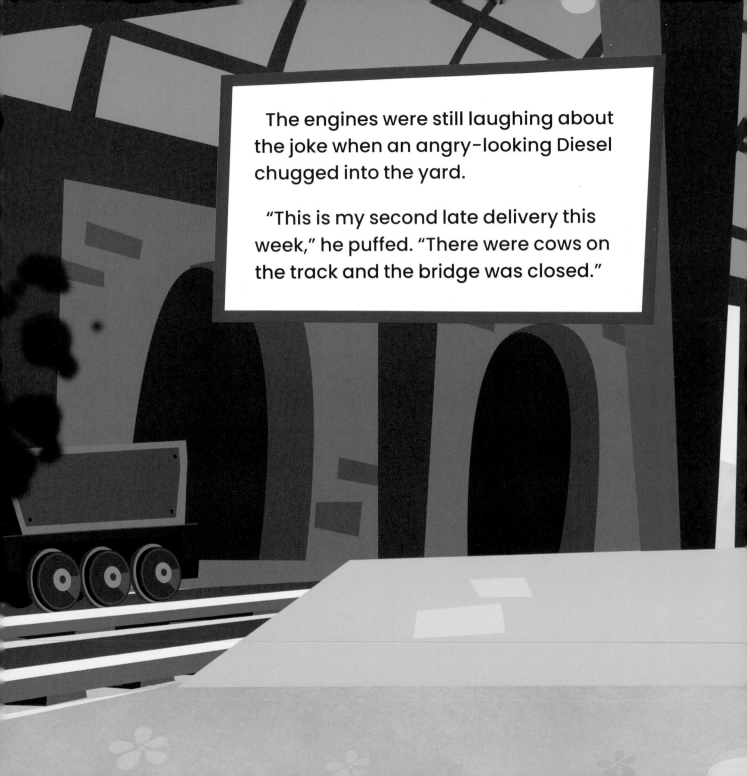

The engines were still laughing about the joke when an angry-looking Diesel chugged into the yard.

"This is my second late delivery this week," he puffed. "There were cows on the track and the bridge was closed."

"It's OK, Diesel," said Thomas kindly. "Everyone is late sometimes."

"Well, I don't want to be!" huffed Diesel.

"I had a late delivery last month and Thomas cheered me up," peeped Percy.

"Yes, all he needed was a laugh!" said Thomas.

Gordon pointed to a second boxcar in the yard.
"Don't worry, Diesel. Try again with your next delivery."

Diesel sighed gloomily and backed up to couple
with the car.

"I've got to deliver this to Brendam Docks by lunchtime," he said and raced off.

Thomas' face fell. "Oh, no! That was another confetti car, only with double the load of confetti," he cried.

"We've got to get Diesel's real delivery to him," said Percy. "He won't be happy if his delivery is late again, especially if he is covered in confetti too!"

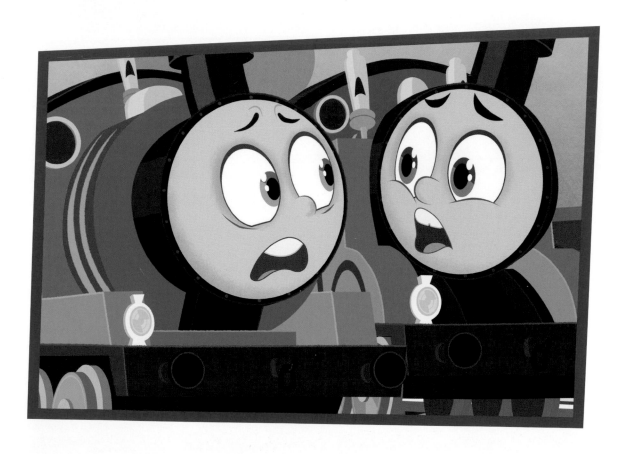

The two little engines raced out of the yard
with Thomas pulling Diesel's real delivery.

"Diesel! Wait!" huffed Percy, as they caught up with him. "There was a mix-up with your delivery."

"That car is going to explode confetti everywhere!" puffed Thomas.

"Confetti? Oh, I get it," muttered Diesel. "You're just pretending to try to cheer me up, but I haven't got time for your jokes."

Before Thomas or Percy could tell him it wasn't a joke, Diesel sped away.

"He doesn't believe us," sighed Percy. "What are we going to do?"

"I'll tell you what we're NOT going to do, we're not going to give up! Diesel's delivery can't be late," declared Thomas, coming to a stop at a track crossing. "We'll block his path."

As Diesel zoomed up to the crossing, seeing the two engines still following him, he pulled a switch and raced off onto another track.

"I told you, I haven't got time for your jokes," he called to them. "I can't be late!"

Finally, the docks were in sight.

"Nothing and no one is going to stop me from making this delivery on time!" Diesel declared. "I'm going to make sure those jokesters can't try to stop me."

Diesel pulled another switch so that Thomas and Percy couldn't follow him down the main track into the docks.

Meanwhile, Thomas and Percy were still trying to catch up with Diesel.

"We've got to get to the docks before Diesel triggers the confetti explosion," said Thomas. "He's nearly there. Quick, this way. I know a shortcut."

Percy looked at the track that cut down to the docks. It was very steep.

"I can do this ... I can do this ... for Diesel!" Percy cried as he dropped over the edge and hurtled down the track. "Ahhhhhhh!"

"We did it!" cheered Thomas, as the two little engines pulled into the docks just ahead of Diesel. "Now we've just got to stop the confetti car exploding."

Diesel chugged up to Thomas and Percy. "Ha! You silly jokesters, you didn't manage to stop me making my delivery on time!"

"Yes, let me take that for you," said Cranky the Crane as he lowered his hook towards the car.

"STOP!" shouted Thomas. "That's not Diesel's delivery ..."

... *BANG! BOOM!*

Clouds of confetti burst out of the car and rained down on all three engines.

Diesel jumped in the air. "What just happened?"

Thomas and Percy looked down sheepishly.

"We're so sorry, we were just trying to help you ..." whispered Thomas.

"Please don't be angry," mumbled Percy.

Diesel looked at his friends' worried faces.

"**HA! HA! HA!**" He burst out laughing. "That was ... hilarious! BEST. JOKE. EVER!"

Thomas and Percy giggled with relief.

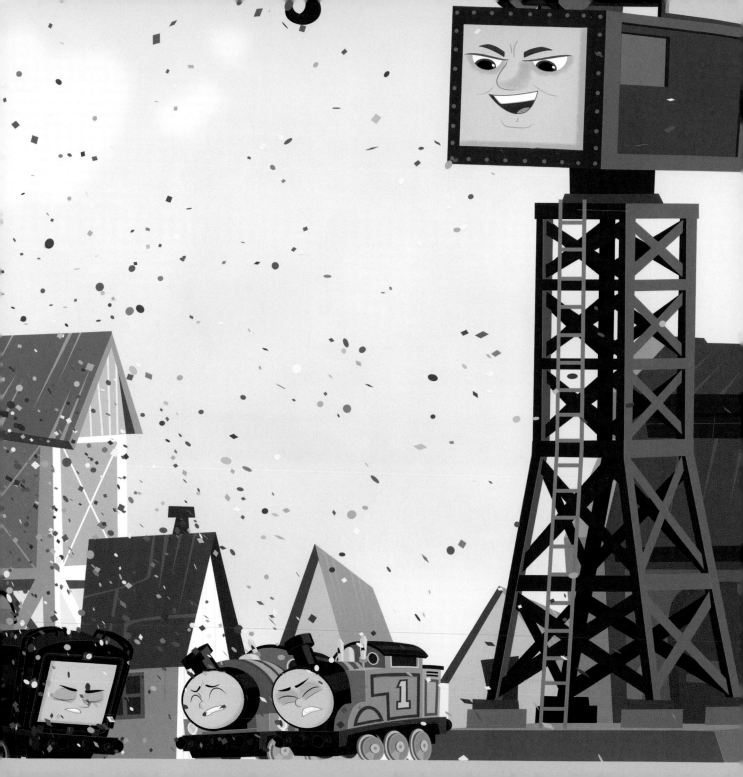

"A good laugh like that can really change your day," chuckled Gordon, arriving at the docks to check on the other engines.

"**TOOT**-ally!" laughed Diesel. "Thanks for cheering me up and making sure my delivery got here on time."

"Anyone want to hear a funny joke …?" giggled Percy.